MW01531213

A REAL JAM

STREET FOOD COZIES, BOOK 11

GRETCHEN ALLEN

SUMMER PRESCOTT BOOKS PUBLISHING

Copyright 2023 Summer Prescott Books

All Rights Reserved. No part of this publication nor any of the information herein may be quoted from, nor reproduced, in any form, including but not limited to: printing, scanning, photocopying, or any other printed, digital, or audio formats, without prior express written consent of the copyright holder.

**This book is a work of fiction. Any similarities to persons, living or dead, places of business, or situations past or present, is completely unintentional.

CHAPTER 1

"I just don't get it," Olivia Mason whispered to her boss's boss. She leaned against the side of the newly remodeled food truck, the eleventh in the fleet, and pointed to the design on the side.

"What don't you get?" Billie Halifax asked. She was not impatient with the younger woman who worked as a sous chef for her barbecue truck manager, Dillon Frazier.

"It's not that these don't taste incredible. They do," Olivia continued. "It's just that every other truck you have here along the boardwalk is special. I mean, Carl doesn't just run a sushi truck. He worked hard to match the menu with the local catch. Both of the bakery trucks serve so much more than just cupcakes and mousse. What they do is absolutely gourmet. I never knew street food could be so unique."

"Thank you," Billie said. "But I don't know what that has to do with the new donut truck."

"It's just… these mini donuts are nothing special," Olivia said. "I can pick up chocolate frosted donuts just like this from a gas station on the mainland for a couple bucks. Same with the cinnamon sugar and powdered sugar varieties. Why is this street food?"

Billie nodded. She expected the same question from Asher Scanlan, her business partner and boyfriend. It was easy to forget that Olivia was once a police officer and not a chef trained at the culinary school on the mainland, her own alma mater, and the source of most of her food truck manager hires.

"Most donut shops offer certain staples," Billie said. She kept her voice low. The last person she wanted to hear the conversation was Cole Rodrigo, the latest addition to the food truck family. He was a trained pastry chef. "Customers expect things like the mini donuts he serves, but he has shown me his specialty menu. He plans to serve a specialty donut called a malasada. You should try one."

"I didn't see those on the menu," Olivia said.

Billie chuckled. "I guess you haven't heard. Cole's menu board was delayed after an accident on the bridge. We decided to open anyway," she explained. She smiled at the younger woman and moved around her. "Hey, Cole!"

"Yeah." A young man stepped into the window. He pushed his wavy black hair away from his eyes and grinned. Billie could almost feel the electricity spark from Olivia. She had to fight the urge to giggle where she stood. She had to admit that Cole was a good-looking young man. Clearly Olivia noticed, too.

"What malasadas do you have ready for me right now?" Billie called back.

"Give me a sec," Cole said. He grinned with his upper lip curled. Had she been younger, and not already enamored with Asher, she might have felt her own knees grow weak. Cole disappeared from the window and returned a second later with a handful of white wax bags, each filled with a special treat. "Okay, so first you've got your mango custard and pina colada fillings. In the middle here is a guava cream filled, and the bottom two are coconut cream and a passion fruit and passion fruit combo." He handed the bag over to Billie and waited.

"What's a, what did you call it?" Olivia asked.

"Malasada," Cole returned to the window and repeated the word more slowly. "Literally means badly baked, which is ironic because there is nothing bad about them. It is a donut variety, Portuguese in origin, but made popular in the islands."

"Which islands?" Olivia asked. She appeared to hang on every word he spoke.

"Hawaiian," Cole said. "I was stationed there for a couple of years while in the service. Since they're Portuguese and so am I, you might say I fell in love with them. I decided to make them my specialty."

"Oh, they're warm," Olivia said. She helped herself to the mango custard variety on top. "Oh, wow! That has a little kick to it, too. What am I tasting?"

"Probably lemon zest," Billie cut in. As entertained as she was by the exchange between them, she had other matters to attend to. The accident two days before on the bridge that delayed the menu board also affected a shipment of supplies she needed for the commissary kitchen she owned with Asher. The kitchen was situated in the middle of several hundred acres on the southern side of Sea Glass Island, their home off the coast of Florida in the Gulf of Mexico. The grounds served as a festival and fair venue for a variety of events all year round. Another festival was set to begin in just a few days.

"I take back what I said before," Olivia said. Her typically somber demeanor had been replaced with something like a teenage school girl with a crush on a boy. Billie was quite sure she knew which one.

"Why don't you stop by later tonight when I prepare a few of them for the rest of the truck managers?" Cole said.

"You mean, when you present your menu?"

Billie shook her head. "He's already done that," she said.

"Yeah, but that was just with you and Asher," Cole said. He turned his attention back to Olivia. "I wanted to get off on the right foot with the rest of the managers, so I thought I would invite everyone over to the commissary kitchen tonight and prepare a feast, so to speak. I guess you'll probably be working, but so will the rest of them. So just stop by when your husband gives you a break from the barbecue truck."

"Husband? Oh, no, Dillon and I aren't married," Olivia said. Her face turned bright red. "We're not anything really. Just friends."

"Ah, good to know," Cole said. He leaned on the counter and gazed at her through the window.

"Alright, you two," Billie said. "Cole is going to make more malasadas when he shuts down for the night. Olivia is going to stop by when she has a break, and then the two of you can get together over the weekend and discuss what you both think of each other. Right now, I have to get back to my office and fix what's broken about the last inventory shipment before the festival starts." She nudged Olivia with her shoulder and offered a knowing wink to Cole, then turned on her heel and headed back toward the beach gate separating the festival grounds from the boardwalk. She could hear the mournful woes of her dog Waffles, the entitled Tibetan Mastiff she'd inherited from Olivia's former love interest, as he wailed in the distance.

"You are about as pitiful as a newborn kitten," Billie muttered under her breath. She reached the large, fenced-in yard where he was waiting for her. His upper half was all that was visible. The rest of him was stretched out inside the extraordinarily large dog house Asher referred to as his "Doggie Mansion."

Given the fact that the dog house was temperature controlled, he was not wrong.

Waffles gazed up at her as she approached. She could tell by the thump-thump coming from inside the doghouse that he fully anticipated a walk, but Billie had other plans. She was determined to grab a fast lunch inside her tiny home and then promptly return to her office in the metal building that housed the commissary kitchen. Waffles would have to wait a few hours for his walk. It wasn't as if she hadn't already taken him down the beach to his favorite spot first thing in the morning.

"You're fine," Billie said when the dog began huffing and puffing. "I'll be back to take you out this evening, Waffles. Don't act like you're the most mistreated dog on the planet right now."

"Do you always speak to animals as if they are human?" Billie turned around in a circle searching for the source of the question. She stopped looking when her eyes rested on a tall man with thinning sandy blond hair standing on the beach in front of her tiny house. He was dressed like a tourist in a white linen suit and baby blue shirt with an open collar.

"I'm sorry," Billie said. "Who are you?"

"Just a visitor." The man smiled. He stepped forward and offered his hand. "Maxwell Martin. And you are?"

"Billie Halifax," she said, not taking his hand. "Owner of the grounds you are standing on. You do know this is private property, don't you?"

"Private property? I thought these were some sort of fairgrounds or something," Maxwell said. His gaze hardened a bit as he spoke.

"Yes, but this place is privately owned," Billie replied. "You're trespassing. We are not open to the public."

"Maybe you should make that more widely known."

"Oh, you mean like the large, metal signs at each and every entrance that state this place is private property? The ones that say 'no trespassing' in bright red letters? I'll be sure to bring that up with my business partner the next time we discuss how to keep the public from invading our business," Billie snapped.

"Explain this to me," he said. He gestured toward the commissary kitchen. "How do you run a festival business by keeping the public out? Isn't that a bit counterintuitive?"

Billie inhaled slowly. She had little patience in general, and even less for the man standing in front of her. "If the gates are open for a festival and you pay to enter, then it isn't trespassing," she said. "See how that works? You pay for the right to be here."

"Okay, so how much is it to be here right now?" Maxwell asked.

Billie forced a smile. "That's the problem," she said. "There isn't an event right now, so you have zero reason to be here. Again, this is private property. So, if you don't mind, please leave the same way you came."

Maxwell shook his head slowly. He raised a finger and shook it at her, as if scolding a small child.

"You're going to wish you hadn't said that to me," he said. "You'll regret being so hasty to push me away."

Billie glared at him as he walked past her tiny house and headed for the beach gate.

CHAPTER 2

"I have no idea who he was," she told Asher thirty minutes later. She stood in the doorframe of his office watching a replay of the video on the security cameras positioned close to her home.

"If you look here, you can see him on the far side of the frame walking around the fifth wheel, between it and your house," Asher said. He held an ink pen close to the computer monitor indicating the grainy image to her. She could tell by the prominent vein in his forehead that he was not happy about the presence of the strange man so close to her tiny house. Billie felt the same. She worried about Polly Sheridan, the young woman who, along with her twin sister Liza, ran the ice cream truck on the boardwalk. What if

Polly had been home alone after dark? Would the man still have trespassed so close to their homes?

"I wish I knew why he was here," Billie said. She waited while Asher slowly moved the video feed. Once a clear image was visible, Asher snapped a screenshot of the man.

"I'm not going to wait around for him to make another appearance," Asher said. He turned around in his chair and waited while the printer started and slowly spit out the photo. "You can go with me, or I can go alone, but that photo is going straight to Sully."

Billie folded her arms over her chest. "Do you think we have enough of a reason to involve Detective Sullivan? I mean, he really didn't do anything but trespass," she said.

"He also left with an ominous warning of sorts," Asher said. "I'm not waiting around for him to show us what he meant by that."

"Fair enough," Billie said. Internally, she was quite relieved by the fact that Asher was going to take it to the police. The man's presence had given her more than a momentary panic. She was still shaken by his sudden appearance behind her.

"In the meantime, I want you to keep these doors

locked when you're here by yourself," Asher instructed.

"Is there something going on that you know about and haven't told me?" Billie asked.

Asher shook his head. "No, but there have been quite a few robberies on the mainland," he said. "Mostly businesses after dark, and I don't want to take any chances."

Billie nodded and stood up straight. She squared her shoulders and brought her hand to her forehead in a salute. "Sir, yes, sir!"

"Alright, smart aleck," Asher said. Billie turned on her heel and marched down the hall toward the kitchen space. He quickly formed a sticky note into a ball and tossed it at her.

When she reached her office, Billie let out a long sigh and sat down. She sighed again and opened her laptop. The task ahead of her was not an easy one. She had pages of kitchen inventory to scroll through and compare to the list she had made weeks ago of what was needed for the upcoming festival.

For the second year in a row, the Florida Craft Show was slated to open on the festival grounds. Billie had referred to her notes from the previous year to compile a list for her food trucks and a general list for the festival in general.

When the multiple-car incident on the bridge shut down traffic for more than eight hours, a delivery van carrying her order was stopped on the mainland and turned back to the warehouse from where it had originated. A phone call from the distributor informed her that her entire order had been returned to stock. After an hour of going around in circles with the office manager, Billie promised to order the same inventory from her other suppliers. The only problem was, she had no reliable supplier to run to. Instead, she was forced to create a list of what was missing and reach out to anyone who could deliver a shipment in less than forty-eight hours.

For the next thirty minutes, Billie called every distributor on her list. Instead of finding a single supplier for her missing items, Billie was forced to arrange the replacement products from three separate warehouses. Her deliveries would begin first thing in the morning. The first truck was scheduled to arrive at seven, and the last delivery was promised by ten the following night.

Billie glanced at the clock on her laptop. She had just under two hours before Cole planned to take over a couple of test kitchen spaces to prepare his homemade malasadas. She was eager to watch his process once again, but the demands of the coming festival threatened to steal away the rest of her evening. And depending on the outcome of Asher's visit with Sully, the sudden intruder on the festival grounds had her thinking about what else might be coming her way.

She had less than two minutes to wonder. A loud knock on the outside door launched her from her seat. She rushed into the hallway and headed for the door. "Billie," Dillon called through the door. "It's Dillon. I need to see you."

Billie flipped the lock on the metal door and pushed it open wide for the manager of the barbecue truck. "What's going on?" she asked.

"Let me inside and shut the door behind us," Dillon said. He looked down the hall past her. "Where is Asher?"

"He had to talk to Sully at the police station," Billie said. She hesitated to fill him in on the rest of the story until she knew more.

"He's with the cops? That's a good thing," Dillon said. He paced up and down the hallway, then turned back to her. "There was some guy clowning around down there asking to come inside the food trucks. He was pushing customers out of the way and even told someone that he owned the taco truck. I don't know if he is some kind of a lunatic or a fraud, but he almost got his face punched in."

Billie listened intently. She knew who he was talking about before she felt the first butterflies swarming in her gut. "Was he tall and dressed in a white suit? Thinning blond hair?" she asked.

"Yeah," Dillon said. His eyes widened. "Do you know this guy?"

"Not personally," Billie said. "But he sounds like the same guy who showed up here just a little while ago. He's the reason Asher met up with Sully in the first place."

"What did he want?" Dillon asked.

Billie shook her head. "I have no idea what he wanted," she explained. "I told him he was trespassing, and he tried to argue with me."

"Let me guess, he told you something like you were going to regret making him leave like that," Dillon said.

Billie nodded. "That's almost exactly what he said to me," she said. "He told me that I was going to regret being so hasty shoving him off."

"Let's call Asher right now," Dillon suggested. "If he's still with Sully, we probably need to let her know he was on the boardwalk."

"On it," Billie said. She ducked into her office and pulled her phone off the desk. She quickly dialed Asher's number and put the phone on speaker.

"Did he come back?" Asher asked as soon as he answered the phone.

"Not here," Billie said. "But Dillon had an interaction with him."

"I'm still with Sully," Asher said. "You're on speaker, man. Tell me what happened."

"Well, it started with him standing in line at the taco truck," Dillon said. "I had gone for a little walk to stretch my legs and I overheard it all. Anyway, when the guy showed up, he waited until it was his turn to order, but the whole time he was looking all around, like he was casing the truck or something. That caught my eye right away."

"Dillon, Sully here," Sully's voice came over the phone speaker. "Was the guy carrying a weapon that you could see?"

"No, but he started quizzing Marcel about how much money the truck makes every day. Marcel was more polite to the man than I would have been," Dillon said. "The guy kept pushing and Marcel asked him five or six times if he would like to order. That's when I ran over and asked Olivia to take over for me for a little while longer."

"Did the man go away at that point?" Sully asked.

"Not at all," Dillon continued. "Marcel politely asked him to move along if he wasn't going to place an order. The guy threw a little fit and walked off. I followed him for a moment. He made his way around to the back of the truck and pushed his way inside."

"What did you do?" Asher asked.

"I helped him back outside," Dillon said.

"After he was removed, what happened?" Sully asked.

Dillon's face hardened. "He headed for Enid's truck, then for the girls' ice cream truck," Dillon said. "I kept my eyes on Olivia and followed him down there. I think that made the guy mad because he started really pushing them to let him inside."

"Please tell me you didn't put your hands on him again," Sully said. Billie swore she could hear her pinching the bridge of her nose as she spoke.

"I did not put my hands on him," Dillon said. He glanced sideways at Billie. "I didn't have to. As soon as he saw me, he started walking around like a caged animal at the zoo. He made some wild claims, too."

"What did he say?" Asher asked.

Dillon lowered his eyes and exhaled slowly before he spoke. "He claimed to be the rightful owner of the trucks," he said.

"Which trucks?" Billie asked.

"All of the trucks," Dillon said. "He said he had

inherited everything from Adeline Lynch, including this building and the grounds."

"He mentioned my grandmother?" Billie asked. She felt the blood drain from her face. "Who is this guy?"

"I don't know, but we'll get to the bottom of things," Sully promised.

CHAPTER 3

"Are we still on for this evening?" Cole asked Billie later in the day. She met him at the back door after sending a group text message to the truck managers that she was going to remain in the commissary kitchen building with the exterior doors locked. She encouraged all of them to text or call ahead if they planned to stop by.

"What does everyone think?" Billie replied to everyone in the group chat. She wanted to hear their thoughts before she shut Cole down.

"I'm for it," Olivia replied. Billie chuckled when she spotted her text first.

"Same," both Sheridan twins responded. Marcel, Enid, Carl, Isa, and Kim quickly agreed, and the other's followed suit shortly after.

"My suggestion is that we all relocate to the festival grounds for the night," Dillon wrote. Billie immediately nodded.

"Let's do that," she texted. "I wish I had thought of that myself. We have no idea where and when his guy is going to show up next. Until the police have the chance to talk to him, I think we can only assume that he is capable of anything."

One by one, each truck manager drove through the front gate and parked their trucks around the back of the building, close to the last remaining unimproved truck. Cole was the first inside and eagerly began mixing the dough for his donuts.

Billie waited for the others to join her, then retrieved a tall stool from the shared kitchen pantry and placed it in front of the counter. As promised, Cole occupied two test kitchens while he prepared his signature donut. Though she wondered why he needed both spaces, it was soon apparent to her that the pastry chef knew exactly what he was doing.

Cole pulled the commercial-size countertop stand-mixers out from both kitchens. On each stove, he brought a small amount of milk nearly to a boil, then shut the fire off and removed the pans. To the slightly cooled milk, he added yeast and sugar.

While the yeast mixture cooled, Cole quickly

added eggs to each mixer and began to beat them at low speed. He moved quickly back and forth between each space. He then dumped a small bag of fresh lemons on the counter and began running each fruit over a handheld grater, zesting the rind.

While Cole measured and added flour, lemon zest, melted butter, sugar, salt, and the cooled yeast to each mixer bowl, Billie watched out of the corner of her eye as Olivia walked around the kitchen space and into the back where the pantry, storage room, and coolers were located. She returned a few moments later with a second stool and set it next to hers.

Cole continued between each mixer. He watched, added more flour, moved to the other kitchen, and watched again for several minutes while the dough hook kneaded each batch into a soft ball. Olivia commented under her breath and asked questions while he worked. Some questions were silly to the ears of the trained chefs in the room, but Cole never once acted as if he was appalled by her queries.

While the dough was rising, the large group sat around getting to know one another better. Polly and Liza pulled a few ice cream samples from the large cooler out and shared them with Cole, who returned a great deal of praise for their efforts.

Olivia remained quiet during the exchange. Cole

turned his attention back to her after several minutes. "I'm really overwhelmed by everything here," he said at last.

"Why do you say it like that?" Marcel asked him.

Cole walked to the other side of the counter in front of Billie and Olivia and leaned on his elbows. "Because you guys are all standing around here waiting for me to share my best dish with you," he said. "Look, I spent time in the service and that was a brotherhood unlike any I have ever known before."

As a veteran himself, Dillon donated a portion of his food truck profits to a local charity he had begun for injured vets. Billie could almost see the respect for the younger man glowing in his eyes.

"But what you guys have got going here is also amazing," he said. "I have a feeling this is just the tip of the iceberg."

"We like to think so," Asher said behind them. He rested his hands on Billie's shoulders and leaned down to whisper in her ear. "Can we talk for a second?"

Billie nodded. "I'll be right back," she announced and slid off her stool. She cast a knowing look in Dillon's direction. He responded with the slightest nod, then launched a new set of questions to Cole about his time in the military.

"Remind me to thank him later," Billie whispered to Asher as they walked down the hall and out the door to the outside.

"Dillon? Yeah, that dude is the best," Asher said. "I feel like he is the real adult in charge around here sometimes."

"You and me both." Billie chuckled. She swallowed hard and gazed up at Asher. "Okay, what is it? You wouldn't bring me out here over nothing. What's going on?"

Asher cleared his throat and walked a few steps down the sidewalk away from her. He turned back and began to speak in very measured words. "The man who was here earlier, Maxwell or whatever his name is? Well, turns out he is sleeping in some sort of camper van in the marina parking lot," he said.

"So, you and Sully located him?" Billie said.

"Yes, Sully, Chief Abernathy, all three of us went there together to talk to the guy and find out what is what," Asher continued. His face turned various shades of red as he spoke. Billie had never seen him so angry in the years they had been together. "Sully walked right up to the door of this van and knocked on it, showed him her badge, and insisted he come right on outside."

"Okay," Billie said doubtfully. "Why do I feel like this doesn't end well?"

"Because it doesn't," Asher said. "As soon as Sully started in on him about who he was and what he was doing here, he pulled out some sort of private investigator's license and started waving it around. So, the questions stopped right there, and they let him go back to his van without another word."

"Wait," Billie said. She was beginning to under-stand why he was so livid. "They just let him go? Even after he trespassed here and forced himself into one of my food trucks?"

Asher planted both hands on his hips and nodded. "Yes," he said. "Yes, they did, but you don't even want to know the rest. I looked inside that van while they were talking. Do you know what I saw?"

"Please don't tell me it was a dead body or some-thing," Billie said.

Asher shook his head. "No, but that at least might have lit a fire under the cops," he said. "What I did see was a bunch of duct tape, rope, and zip ties."

Billie closed her eyes and inhaled. "That's not ominous or anything," she said, shaking her head.

"Right? That's what I said. I pointed it out to the chief and to Sully," he said. "But do you know what they did? They asked him what those items were for.

They asked him! I would have had that idiot in handcuffs so fast his head would have been spinning all the way off the island and to jail."

"What did he say?" Billie asked. Her heart raced in her chest. "What reason did he have for having all of that?"

Asher chuckled and shook his head. "He said he was going exploring a little later. Claimed there was some sort of cave off the south shore that he wanted to check out," he said. "The worst part is that Sully and the chief bought what he had to say! They left him there and told me on the way back to leave the guy alone."

"Yet he claims he owns this place and these food trucks," Billie said. She was beyond exasperation. "How could they let him go knowing that?"

"Max or Maxwell or whoever he is denied he ever said that," Asher said. His jaw tensed as he spoke. "I don't like this, Billie. I don't like it one bit."

"I'm not a big fan of it either, but what do you propose we do about it?"

"For one thing, we aren't going to take any chances around here," Asher said. "I want the gates and the doors to remain locked at all times. You need to tell your managers to communicate with you when they are coming and going."

"Already done," Billie said. "Maybe it's a good thing that this craft show starts in a couple of days. We'll just move all of the food trucks on the festival grounds for the event. That's four days."

"Yes, but that's also four days this clown will be able to come and go around here freely," Asher said. "I'm going to make sure all the cameras are working and double check the locks on everything."

Billie felt a shiver run through her. "What do you think is going to happen?"

Asher shook his head again. "I don't know, Billie," he said. "But I have a feeling those zip ties had nothing to do with cave exploration and everything to do with what this guy is really after."

CHAPTER 4

When Billie returned to the commissary kitchen, Cole had begun dividing the dough into equal parts. He rolled each piece out into a little disc, then placed each disc on a small piece of waxed paper on the counter.

While the malasadas continued to rise for another ten or fifteen minutes, Cole lit the fire under a pair of cast iron Dutch ovens on each stove. He poured oil in each and turned his attention back to the dough.

Billie noticed the cooling racks he had set up on the far side of the second kitchen. Two large glass bowls filled halfway full of confectioner's sugar were set between the racks and two metal sheet pans.

"It only takes about forty-five seconds on each side once you place them in the oil," Cole explained.

He began adding one donut at a time to the oil. He raced back and forth between the kitchen spaces.

"Would you like an extra hand?" Olivia asked. She practically came off her stool when she asked.

"Are you trained?" Cole asked her.

"Nope," Olivia said, walking confidently around the counter and into the kitchen. "But I can take direction like nobody's business. Just show me what to do."

While Cole gave Olivia a quick tutorial, Billie watched as Asher pulled Dillon away from the kitchen space. The pair walked down the hall toward Asher's office. She didn't have to guess what the topic of discussion might be.

"Billie," Cole called out. "Would you mind running to the cooler for me? I forgot the filling for these that I made earlier today."

"Sure," Billie said, sliding off her stool. "What does it look like?"

"It's in a large, glass dish with a white lid," Cole said. "I put it on one of the middle racks just a step or two inside the smaller cooler in the back."

Billie smiled and nodded. She walked around behind the kitchens and into the back. The filling was easy to spot. She fought the temptation to pull the lid off and taste test some of it herself. Instead, she carried the glass bowl to the front and set it on the counter where Cole indicated.

"This is traditional haupia custard filling." Cole produced a pastry bag and started spooning large scoops of the filling into it as he spoke. "It's a simple custard mixture made over low heat with milk, egg yolks, cornstarch, and sugar. Once the mixture boils, you want to add coconut milk until it's thick, but don't let it boil again. Then take it off the heat and add in pure vanilla extract and coconut flavoring for an extra rich flavor."

"That sounds complicated," Olivia said. She turned another small batch of the pastries onto the cooling racks and added three more to the oil.

"It's hard until you learn how to make custard," Enid added.

"Right. I burned through so many batches of custard my first year in school." Polly chuckled.

Billie glanced at Olivia. Her face had darkened slightly. Billie wondered if she felt inadequate surrounded by culinary school alumni.

"You are a natural at that, Liv," Billie said. Her comment elicited a smile from Olivia.

"That's the last of them," Olivia announced to Cole. "What's next?"

"Well, if you really want to help out, take the

malasadas we made first and start rolling them in the sugar, then set them on the pans so I can fill them."

"As you wish, boss," Olivia said. Billie cringed inwardly for her.

Despite the awkwardness of the obvious love fest between them, Cole and Olivia worked well in tandem. As soon as Olivia placed a warm donut on the tray, Cole picked it up and expertly piped the filling into it. When the first tray was finished, Asher and Dillon returned from the office and gathered around the counter again.

"Do I need to start looking for a new sous chef, Olivia?" Dillon asked.

"Oh, no," Olivia said. Her face reddened again. "Not at all. I'm just helping out. And learning a lot as I go."

"I don't know," Cole said. "I haven't really worked with an assistant before, but I like this system. You might need to start hunting for some help after all."

"You could help Cole early in the morning and me a little later," Dillon offered. Billie caught the humor in his countenance. He was teasing his younger assistant.

"I can? Are you sure that's okay?" Olivia asked.

She clasped her hands in front of her chest, closely resembling a delighted teenage girl.

Asher chuckled and turned his head. Dillon's teasing had backfired on him. "I mean, sure," Dillon replied. "As long as you're okay with all of that extra time on your feet, Liv."

Olivia nodded her head. "I want to do this with Cole," she blurted out. Her face was instantly red again. "I mean, I want to learn from him, too. This pastry stuff is very interesting to me."

"I bet," Carl muttered.

"Stick to sushi, fish boy," Olivia shot back.

"Alright, everyone," Billie cut in. "I want to try one of these malasadas."

Cole immediately plated one and set it on the counter in front of her. Billie picked it up and slowly bit into the still warm pastry. "Oh, that's amazing," she said. Her eyes closed as she savored the sweet coconut filling. "I'm in absolute awe."

"Yeah, me too," Enid said. "This is not what I was expecting when you said you were adding a donut truck to the fleet."

"Same," Marcel said. He stuffed half of a malasada into his mouth. "I was thinking of glazed, chocolate sprinkles."

"That's why we went with the mini donut

makers," Cole said. "The machines pretty much run themselves and the labor to prepare them isn't too intense. Billie made sure the truck has two small fryers so I can whip up the dough here each morning then continue making fresh malasadas all day."

"Speaking of which, I'm going to have to call it a night," Enid stood up and announced.

"Me, too." Dillon nodded toward Asher. "Polly? Can I walk you to your trailer?"

"Sure," Polly said. She cast a glance at Billie. "Is there a reason we still need to be cautious?"

Billie stood up from her seat and walked over to where Asher stood. "I guess you all need to hear this right now," she said. "You all are aware of the troublemaker from earlier today."

"Well, he's more than just an intruder," Asher said. He picked up a stack of papers with the man's photo from the table behind him and handed half of them off to Dillon. "Take one of these from Dillon or me and keep an eye out for this creep."

"Do we really need to be that worried?" Cole asked.

Olivia took the photo and nodded. "What did the chief have to say about this?" she asked. Gone was her sweet, schoolgirl voice. Her old cop persona seemed to take over.

"The chief, along with Detective Sullivan, questioned him earlier today," Billie said. "He is a licensed private investigator so that apparently affords him some leeway with the cops."

"Only thing is, he denied claiming he was the rightful owner of Billie's property when they questioned him," Asher cut in. "Let me tell you, the dude is up to no good. Sully and the chief wouldn't search his camper van, but I got a good look inside. If I'm not mistaken, the guy had a kidnapper's starter kit laying out right there in the open."

"That's reassuring," Liza muttered.

"Until further notice, we need to park the trucks here every night," Dillon directed. "That won't be hard over the coming days with the new festival starting, but we need to be safe. I'm sorry if this sounds wrong, but that means that the guys need to keep a special eye out for the ladies. We have no idea what this creep is up to or what he may do."

"Have we looked into the guy yet?" Olivia asked.

"That's what Dillon and I were looking into a little while ago," Asher said.

"We came up with absolutely nothing," Dillon interjected. "I mean, there was nothing on a Maxwell Martin anywhere we had access to. Not even an advertisement for his investigative services. Nothing."

"That makes me even more worried," Olivia said.

"Why is that?" Cole asked her.

"Because if the guy is a ghost online, that probably means Maxwell Martin is not his real name, and if he's here under a pseudonym, you can guarantee he's up to no good."

CHAPTER 5

Billie waited until the last of her truck managers left and then waited for Asher to finish reassuring himself that the feed from the security cameras was synced with his cell phone. He insisted on walking her the short distance to her tiny house.

"I'll let you know before I take Waffles out in the morning," Billie said when they reached her front door.

"Maybe you shouldn't go anywhere," Asher said. "It's not safe. I just have this gut feeling."

Billie sighed. "I know what you're saying, but the dog has to be walked," she said. "You could go with me."

Asher shook his head. "I wish, but first thing

tomorrow morning, the grounds crew is going to be here to get everything going for the craft fair."

Billie slapped her palm against her forehead. "I have deliveries coming in all day, too," she said. "Thanks to the bridge shutting down a couple of days ago, I had to order replacements from three separate distributors."

"I'll be here to handle that for you," Asher said. "Why don't you wait until the sun is up and then take Waffles around the boardwalk for his morning exercise? Stay away from the southern part of the island and just walk him around the beach in full view of the boardwalks and the shops."

"So annoying," Billie said wryly. She needed the quiet early morning walks as much as Waffles did, especially on the far southern beach where there were far fewer people early in the mornings.

"Billie," Asher said.

"I know, I know," she interrupted. "What you're suggesting makes sense and I will stick to the beach closer to home. It's just that there's a festival about to start and I need my alone time."

"You have keys to the houseboat," Asher said. "If you need a break, run over there and take an hour or so to yourself."

"Thanks for that," Billie said, thankful he had

decided to keep his houseboat for a while longer, rather than getting a tiny house like her. She said goodnight to him and waited while he made his rounds to check on the fifth wheel parked next to her house, where Polly was asleep. She slipped into the shower and then snuggled beneath her covers thirty minutes later.

Thanks to the excitement of the day, Billie fell fast asleep. She was exhausted from the added stress of the intruder and the news of his ability to slither out of suspicion with the local police. Around three in the morning, she woke with a start to the sound of Waffles growling loudly. She sat straight up in bed and immediately texted Asher. Before he even had a chance to answer, Polly had already texted her.

"Something is outside," Polly wrote.

"Asher knows," Billie replied. She glanced at his return text on her phone and reassured Polly that he was on his way over. "I'm going to have a quick look myself."

"You should wait for Asher," Polly responded. "Please be careful."

Billie set the phone down on her night stand where it was plugged into the charger. She slipped into her clothes and put on her shoes, then carefully stepped outside on her front deck. She gazed out into the darkness but could see nothing. She walked noise-lessly down the steps and stepped on the soft white sand below. She walked toward the front of her tiny house and peered around the side. She could see the nose of the fifth wheel.

Nothing appeared out of the ordinary. She walked back around to the rear side of her tiny house. Asher appeared in the darkness behind her. "What are you doing?" he asked.

"Just checking on things out here," she said. "Whatever the noise was woke Waffles up. He's not growling any longer, though. I suppose it might have been a rodent or something."

"Or a snake," Asher said.

"I try to forget that there are snakes on this island," Billie said.

"If you stay clear of the grassy areas, you usually can forget it," Asher said. "Anyway, you go on back inside and let me have another look outside here. I will be inside in a second. We need to take a look at the security footage when I come inside."

Billie nodded and headed back around the front and stopped cold. "Asher," she shouted out in the darkness. The figure of a man stood in the shadows about ten feet from the front of her tiny house. He was dressed in dark clothing and his face was covered. She couldn't see who he was, but she was quite sure she knew.

Asher raced around the back of the tiny house. Billie said nothing but pointed in the direction the figure had gone. He took off running after him. Billie rushed back inside her house. She swiped her phone off the night stand in her room and called the police.

Asher returned a few minutes later. "I lost him," he said, breathing hard.

"The cops should be here any second," Billie said.

"Good, because there was definitely somebody out there," Asher said. He turned her phone screen to her and held it while she watched. The camera was positioned on the far corner of the commissary kitchen. Both the fifth wheel and the tiny house were visible but in the darkness, the image was grainy. Still, the figure was clearly visible.

"The only problem is that we can't tell who it actually is," Billie said.

"I don't think there is any doubt," Asher said.

"I don't either, but we can't prove anything," Billie said. She looked out the window. "The police are here."

"Come on in," Asher said, opening the door.

"What's the problem?" an officer asked before he

walked inside. "We got a call that there was a disturbance."

"And your front gate was locked up tight," another officer complained. Billie was slightly familiar with the first officer but had not yet met the second. Both were recent recruits from a mainland police academy.

"We had to do that because of an intruder I discussed with the chief and Detective Sullivan earlier," Asher said.

"Okay, and you had another sighting tonight?"

Billie stepped forward. "I was asleep when my dog woke me up, growling," she said. "He never growls like that. Anyway, because of the issues we had with the trespasser both here on the festival grounds and down on the boardwalk earlier, I called Asher right away."

"Are you the only one who heard anything?"

"My neighbor in the fifth wheel did as well," she said. "Her name is Polly Sheridan, and she is also an employee of mine. She texted me that she heard something too."

"That dog may have been spooked by any number of things," the first cop said.

"I saw someone," Billie said. "I saw a man

standing about ten feet in front of my house." She pointed in the direction she had seen the dark figure.

"Are you sure you saw something?"

Billie nodded. She tried to hide her growing annoyance at the police officers' attitudes. "We have it on security video," she said. "The figure is not hard to see."

Asher wordlessly started the video again for the two of them to see. Both police officers watched the footage. Neither said a word. "As you can see, there was clearly someone wandering around here," Asher said. "And he was obviously dressed so no one would recognize him."

"All I see is someone running around here in dark clothes," the first officer said, still standing in the front doorway.

"What's going on?" Sully asked behind him.

"We had an intruder," Billie announced over the heads of the two responding officers. "I saw him, and the cameras captured his image."

"Here, Sully," Asher said. He started the video over and handed it to her through the two officers. Sully took the phone from him and watched it while she stood on the sand in front of the tiny house.

"Okay," Sully said and handed the video back. "Someone was clearly trespassing."

"I think we know who that is," Asher said.

"There is no way to prove it," Sully said. "I think you guys can understand why my hands are tied at this point, but what we will do is increase patrols around this area."

"Are you going to go back to the marina parking lot and question him?" Billie asked.

Sully sighed. "Officers, could you please allow me access here?" She waited while they officers stepped out of the way. "Why don't the two of you go ahead and conduct a perimeter search?"

"Yes, ma'am," the first officer said.

"Okay, I think we both know who the intruder likely was," Sully said. "But for the time being, there is no reason for me to approach Maxwell Martin."

"Come on, Sully!" Asher shouted. "What in the world is going on here? You know us. You know we wouldn't tell you a bunch of nonsense. Several of our people have had run-ins with this guy. He all but threatened Billie and several of the truck managers. We all know who was here wandering around tonight. What is it going to take for you to take this seriously?"

"I do take this seriously, Asher," Sully said. She turned around and made sure she was alone, then lowered her voice and continued, "Listen, this guy is an expert. Somehow, he's pushing it right to the edge, but not doing anything that's enough for us to take him in. If he is up to something, we are going to have to make sure we proceed very carefully."

"So, what do we do now?" Billie asked. "Do you want me to do like Asher said and just wait for this man to hurt me or one of my employees?"

"Of course not," Sully said. "Guys, I am not the enemy here. My hands are tied until we have more to go on."

"You know what I saw when I looked inside that van," Asher said. "How long do we have to wait until this guy proves he is not just carrying around duct tape and zip ties for recreational activities?"

CHAPTER 6

Billie woke early the following morning. For a moment, she had forgotten about the threat from the night before, but as soon as she spotted Asher sleeping on her couch, she remembered. After Sully and the two officers left, Asher had insisted on staying close by with his phone set to alert him if the security cameras picked up any more movement.

As far as Billie knew, nothing more had happened overnight. She moved carefully around the tiny house and readied herself for her morning walk with Waffles. Instead of their typical walk on the southern, less populated beaches, she planned to take Waffles for a walk close to the boardwalk as she had promised Asher she would do.

"You heading out?" Asher emerged from his sleep and stood up, scratching his head and eyes after a long night.

"Yeah," Billie said. "I'll stick to the path we discussed. I slept like a rock for a couple of hours after Sully left. Did you see anything else on the cameras?"

Asher laughed and plopped down on the couch. "I think I woke up about every thirty minutes with a new alert," he said. "Turns out there were no more strangers in the darkness, just a few critters running around in the sand outside."

"I suppose that's a good thing," Billie said. "Not that you didn't have a good night of rest, but that there were no dark-clothed strangers lurking around again."

"Yeah, that's for sure," Asher said.

Billie checked her cell phone and shoved it into the pocket of her yoga pants and leaned down to kiss him on top of the head. "Why don't you sleep for a little while longer?" she suggested. "My phone is fully charged. If I see or hear anything, I'll call the cops first and you second."

"After last night, you might want to call me first and them second," Asher said.

"Maybe, but I don't think Sully was dismissive of us last night," Billie said. "I honestly think she is limited by what she can do. This Maxwell Martin guy is slick."

"Of course, call the police first, babe," Asher said. "But your best bet is to stick close to populated areas."

"Good thing that is exactly what I intend to do." She flashed a smile in his direction and headed outside with the leash in her hand. "You ready, buddy?" She opened the gate to the dog pen and waited for the extra-large pooch to finish stretching. Instead of his typical tail-wagging self, even Waffles looked exhausted from the night before.

Billie hooked the leash onto his dog collar and waited for him to stand up fully and head out of the gate. Waffles walked slowly toward the fifth wheel. It wasn't until they reached the gate that it seemed to dawn on him that they were not headed to the south beach. He strained against the leash a little bit and whined as they walked toward the boardwalk. Billie held firm and guided him down to the beach. The sun was barely up. The beach was practically empty, though there were more people than she normally saw on their usual walks.

It was odd to see the boardwalk empty of the food trucks since all eleven of them were locked away safely behind the gates on the festival grounds. She could see a few lights burning in the shops beyond the boardwalk. The Sea Glass Island Community Center was one of them, and her friend Rhonda Knapp was surely already there.

Waffles picked up his pace the second he noticed the water lapping against the sandy shoreline. Billie had to pull him back a bit when he began splashing and playing in the water. He yelped and jumped up as high as the leash would allow when two crabs walked out of the waves and skittered toward him.

"I can't let you off the leash, buddy," Billie said. She looked around and exhaled slowly. She spotted a dozen or so women walking on the beach. No men were in sight. Not that she had an issue seeing men on the beach, but there was no one who even closely resembled Maxwell Martin.

After wrestling with the leash and the determined dog on the other end, Billie decided to turn Waffles back toward the boardwalk. She led him along the beach away from the water toward the start of the shops on the other side.

"Good morning," Rhonda called to her from the sandy area on the other side of the building. "I'm not used to seeing the two of you on this side of the beach!" She was seated on a weathered bench with a cup of coffee in her hand.

"There was an issue last night," Billie said when she got closer. "We had an intruder problem."

"I heard a little bit about that," Rhonda said. "Who is this guy?"

"This guy is the rightful owner of the food trucks and that large plot of land over there," a man's voice interrupted their conversation. Billie gasped when she saw Maxwell Martin in front of her.

"What are you doing here?" she demanded. Waffles growled at her feet and Billie held on tight to the leash.

"I think you need to move along, sir," Rhonda stood up and said. She gestured toward the beach with her coffee cup.

Maxwell laughed. "I think you'll find that is something I don't do very well," he said. "I don't move along. I won't go away. I go after what I want and don't stop until I get what I came for."

"You know," Billie said. Her nerves stood on end as she spoke. "I think you're threatening me again, Mr. Martin. I don't appreciate that. In fact, I think I need to call the police."

"You better not do that," Maxwell said. Billie was

chilled by the smile on his face. "I am the rightful owner of the food trucks you have hidden behind the gates to the festival grounds. I am the one who has a rightful claim to everything Adeline left you."

Rhonda tossed the contents of her coffee mug on the sand below her and scoffed. "How in the world are you in any way entitled to this woman's property left to her by her own grandmother?"

"Because Adeline is not her grandmother," Maxwell said. "She is mine, and now I am here for what is rightfully my own. I will get it." His eyes nearly bugged out of his head as he spoke. He shook and his voice raised.

"How do you figure that?" Rhonda said. Her eyes were wide with confusion.

"Who in the world do you think you are, lady?" Maxwell asked. He walked closer to them. Billie's hands began to shake as she fiddled with her phone.

Rhonda stood up to him, unfazed by his threatening posture. "I was Adeline's best friend. For years. And I knew this woman when she was a youngster," she said. "I know her face. I know her mother and her father, but I don't know you. I have never seen nor heard of you in my entire life. You're not Adeline's grandson. Who are your parents?"

Billie held her phone up and dialed the police. With a smile on his face, Maxwell Martin leaned over and knocked the phone out of her hands. It fell on the ground in front of her. "No, no," he said. "You should not have done that. I told you before that this is the way things are going to go from now on. The best and the safest thing for you and your friends to do is to simply give up and give me what is rightfully my own."

Rhonda shook her head and laughed in disbelief. "I don't understand for one minute where this is coming from," she said. "I knew Adeline. I have never even seen you before. Tell me this, what did Adeline look like? Can you describe her to me?"

"I don't have to answer your questions," Maxwell snapped.

"Okay, but you can and will answer the questions of an attorney," Rhonda said. She pulled her own phone out and scrolled through her contacts until she found Alex's phone number. "Alex Regent is not only Adeline's former attorney, but the executor of her will."

"Shut up," Maxwell said. He reached out and grabbed Rhonda's phone, taking it from her. Billie reached down for her own phone, but Maxwell took a step toward her. His shadow fell over her. "If you touch that phone, you aren't going to like what happens."

"I think you better back up now, buddy." Billie looked up to see Dillon standing behind him. "Lay a hand on her and you won't walk again for a month. That's a promise."

Maxwell turned around and faced him. Billie stood up with her phone in her hand. She looked down and noticed that the call had gone through. She put the phone to her ear.

"Billie! What is going on there?" Sully yelled into the phone.

"It's Maxwell Martin," Billie said.

"Where are you?" Sully asked.

"At the far end of the shops," Billie said quietly. "He threatened me and Rhonda. Dillon is here with him now."

"I heard enough," Sully said. "I'm on my way."

"The police are coming," Billie said. She turned her phone around and covertly turned on the camera.

Maxwell turned around to her and sneered. The camera captured his image perfectly. He turned back to Dillon and squared his shoulders for a second, but then took off running toward the beach. He threw Rhonda's phone in the sand as he ran.

"Should I try to stop him?" Dillon asked.

"No," Billie said. "That could give him a case against you in court."

"Billie," Rhonda said. Her bemused look had been replaced by wide-eyed horror. "Whoever that guy is, you need to be careful. There is something scary about him. He is the epitome of evil."

CHAPTER 7

"I'm calling Alex," Rhonda said. She dusted the sand off her phone and pressed it to her ear as they walked back to her storefront.

"What happened out there?" Sully asked while Rhonda placed her phone call.

Billie collapsed onto the stool that she had sat in many times over since her move to Sea Glass Island. "I was just out for a walk with Waffles," she said. "I spotted Rhonda in the distance and decided to come say hi to her. We were talking when Maxwell walked up to us and started laying down threats."

"Threats?"

"Yes, threats," Billie said. She felt the anger boiling inside.

"Did he say what he wanted?" Sully asked.

"My life," Billie said. "He claims he owns everything my grandmother left to me. The food trucks, the festival grounds, the commissary kitchen, all of it. He said I'm not her granddaughter, but he is her grandson."

"And how did Rhonda get involved?" Sully continued to write in her small notepad as Billie spoke.

"You mean aside from the fact that he threatened her as well? She bravely told him he was full of it because she knew my grandmother," Billie said. Tears filled her eyes. "She was her best friend. She remembers me from when I was little, too. Never once had she ever mentioned some other guy by the name of Maxwell Martin. He wouldn't even tell who his parents were! My father was an only child."

"Okay, and as far as you know, there were no other children?" Sully asked.

"No! Not only were there no other kids hiding out somewhere, but my grandmother also left these things to me legally through her attorney," Billie shouted. She was at the end of her patience.

"What did he do to you?"

"Slapped my phone out of my hand," Billie said.

"Did Rhonda see him do this?" Sully asked.

"Yes, Rhonda saw the whole thing," Rhonda called from behind the counter.

"Okay," Sully said. She folded her notepad over and tucked it into the pocket of her pants. "I have four officers out looking for him. As soon as he's found, he'll be brought in. Maybe we can get to the bottom of this mess before the festival starts."

"Billie," Asher rushed through the door just then. "What happened?"

"Maxwell happened," Billie said.

"I'll let her fill you in," Sully said when Rhonda came back over to them. "This goes for all of you. Be vigilant, folks. This guy is slick. He doesn't seem to have a whole lot to lose, either."

"Now you think he's a threat? What about last night when we spotted him on our security cameras?" Asher asked. "Or the other night when he told Billie she was going to regret making him leave? Or how about the kidnapper's starter kit we saw inside his camper van down by the marina?"

"No, Asher," Sully said. "It's now that I have something I can legally go with. You and I both understand how the law works in these cases."

"If everyone can calm down for a moment, I have some news," Rhonda said.

"What's going on?" Billie asked. She was

exhausted from the night before and from the tension between Asher and Sully.

"Alex will be here by noon," Rhonda announced. "He has no idea who Maxwell Martin is and says there is no legal claim against your grandmother's estate or your inheritance. He's having his staff look into any other claims or correspondence but says he's not aware of anything."

"He's not worried about any legitimacy to these claims?" Sully asked.

"Not even close," Rhonda said. "He called some of Billie's family while I was on the phone with him and got a very definitive answer from them, too. There is no long lost son. There is nothing in this guy's claims that even deserves a second thought."

"Go back to the kitchen and stay close to each other," Sully instructed. She ignored Asher's glare. "Tell your truck managers to watch out for each other, too. In fact, if you can keep them close by, I would. You might have better luck keeping them on the festival grounds where you can keep an eye on things with the security cameras than down here on the boardwalk."

Asher stood and saluted, then stalked outside. He grabbed the leash and guided Waffles down the wooden sidewalk.

"I'd better go," Billie said. She cast a weary smile at Sully and stood up.

"I'll stop by a little bit later and check in on you," Rhonda said. "I just have a few things to do here and then I'll close up shop for the day."

"What time do you think you'll be over?" Billie asked.

"No later than eleven," Rhonda said. "I expect you to have a feast of some kind ready for me for lunch when I arrive."

Billie smiled and tossed a kiss in Rhonda's direction. She pushed the door open and rushed down the sidewalk where Asher was waiting for her with the dog. He switched the leash into his right hand and circled his left arm around her shoulders.

"Before you say anything, I'll call and apologize to Sully later," he promised. "I know I lost my cool back there."

"You did," Billie said. She snuggled closer to him as they walked. "And I know why you did. I think Sully gets it, too."

"I don't really care if she gets it or not. I still have to make it right," Asher said. "Even if I'm still upset about all of this."

"You heard what she said," Billie replied. "Her hands were tied, legally speaking."

"I understand," Asher said. "But you and I have both seen her bend the rules before. She does it, ever so slightly, when it suits her purposes. I just don't understand why she is being so unyielding about it this time."

"Why is it bothering you so much though?"

"Because this time is affects you directly. More than ever before and that scares me, Billie. I can barely think straight."

CHAPTER 8

"Can we just operate here for the day?" Enid asked Billie from her seat in the commissary kitchen. The truck managers were gathered together for the second time in twenty-four hours. This time, the occasion was far less festive than sampling the exotic donuts made by their latest team member.

"That's what the police are advising us to do," Billie said. She stood in the center of the middle kitchen pouring coffee into cups for each of them. Cole had already begun his preparations for the day in another space.

"At least if we're parked inside the festival grounds, we can keep an eye on things by camera," Asher said. "Dillon, I know you have a truck to run yourself, but if you can park on the far end near the back gates, I would appreciate your help keeping an eye on things."

"This feels like we're circling the wagons," Olivia said. "I know I wasn't the best cop in the world, but what we're doing is probably the safest thing we can do, short of shutting down."

"None of us want that," Marcel added. "Although I would suggest locking up your trucks, even while you're inside."

"Dillon, I'll come by and relieve you at the top of every hour so you can do a quick walk around," Billie announced.

"Let me park on the other end," Cole suggested. He set a large ball of dough in an oiled bowl with a loud plop. "I'm doing as much prep work as I can right now so I can keep an extra eye out as well. I have military training, too. Might as well put it to some use here."

"What difference does military training make?" Thomas asked. As one of the newest truck managers, he rarely spoke up.

"Just that we are trained a little bit more than the average person to keep an eye out for trouble," Dillon gently explained. "Once you have that sort of training, it becomes second nature. I think if we're all watching, we can report anything that is out of place."

"What we need is to keep an eye out for this clown Maxwell Martin," Asher said. "You all have a picture of him already. Later today, the lawyer who hired each of you is due to arrive. He will put an end to any of this guy's nonsense once and for all."

"I sure hope so," Dillon said. "The vendors from the craft fair should start arriving tomorrow."

"Right, so we may have to relocate the trucks according to the festival map Asher developed with the promoters," Billie said. "But for today, we're going to circle the wagons together and keep an eye out for this lunatic." She cast a knowing look at Olivia and headed back to her office.

"Can I help you out this morning?" Asher poked his head in to ask. "Your first delivery is in the pantry, but I haven't touched a single box."

Billie smiled at him from her desk. "I was just coming in here for the order list so I could get busy with that myself," she said. "I won't turn down any help because I think most of my day is going to be spent helping out others here and there, starting with the barbecue truck."

"You probably ought to nail down the menu for lunch, too," Asher said with a smile. "When Rhonda says she wants lunch, we both know she expects the five-star treatment."

Billie nodded. She snatched the list from under her laptop and quickly scanned it into her printer to make a copy for Asher. "I think we've spoiled that woman beyond repair," she said. "I should go ahead and put an order in now for steak and sushi."

"I hope that's just for starters," Asher joked. He grabbed his copy out of her hands and started down the hall toward the kitchen expanse.

"I'm going to need gallons of strong coffee today," Billie said as they passed Cole in the kitchen.

"I have a pot started," Cole said. "I made it extra strong, too."

"Thank goodness." Billie smiled. "We'll be in the pantry for now."

"I'll let you know when it's ready," Cole called after them.

Asher was quiet when they made their way around the back of the kitchen area. He followed her around to the storage room first and shut the door behind them. "What did Alex tell you about Cole?" he asked.

"Cole? Just that he was a veteran and an experienced pastry chef," Billie said. She plucked a box knife off the shelf in front of her and turned to face him. "Why are you asking me about Cole? You were part of the interview process with him, too."

"Yeah, but there's something bothering me," Asher said. "I just find it ironic that this Maxwell Martin guy showed up in town around the same time as Cole. I mean, we don't know anything about him, really. Maybe he's somehow involved with this guy."

Billie shook her head. "Where is this coming from?" she asked. "Tell me one thing he has done that is suspicious?"

"I can't," Asher said. "It has nothing to do with anything he has said or done, aside from his offer to watch the other end of the gates. He doesn't know Dillon from Carl. Why would he just speak up and offer to keep an eye out for this guy? Maybe he's a lookout or something."

"Or maybe he's a vet just like Dillon is, a fact I just told you. You know how ex-military guys are. They have a brotherhood we can't understand."

"Yeah, it just seems like odd timing to me," Asher said.

"I think you have that backwards, Asher," Billie said. "Cole's arrival date was planned six weeks ago. Maxwell Martin just showed up out of the blue a few days ago."

"About the same time Cole arrived," Asher said.

"Coffee's ready," Cole called from the kitchen.

"Don't say anything to him right now," Billie said. "If you're nervous, why don't you quietly ask Sully to look into him on her end? He won't be any the wiser if you keep it quiet."

"Very clever," Asher said. "You just said that so I have to make up with Sully, though, right?"

"Hey, you're the one acting all suspicious and crazy about one of my truck managers," Billie said. "I didn't bring this up." She opened the door to the storage room and headed for the pantry with the box knife and the list.

Two hours later, Billie emerged with an aching back and a renewed sense of calm. She was grateful that the first of her three orders was put away. She glanced at the clock. Rhonda was due to arrive soon, and she had a gourmet lunch to put together.

Cole had left the kitchen for his food truck already. Billie considered utilizing one of the kitchens to prepare a meal herself, but with the second order due to arrive anytime, she settled for an eclectic spread from her food trucks. After a quick text to Marcel and Olivia, Billie headed outside.

Ten minutes later, Billie was back inside the commissary kitchen area. She set the food on a table in the seating area, then headed to the storage room for a set of real dishes. She decided to treat Rhonda like a guest at a four-star restaurant with the best white serving platter and matching place setting that she could find.

She arranged the smoked brisket nachos, the collaboration between the barbecue truck and Marcel's taco truck, on the platter and waited. Rhonda would arrive any moment, throw her hands back at the presentation and declare Billie a show-off for it.

"What time was she supposed to be here?" Asher asked twenty minutes later. Billie had placed the platter in a warming oven and taken to watching for her friend outside. She stood just outside the metal door close to her office and watched for any sign of Rhonda. A few minutes later, she informed Asher that she was going to take a walk across the sand toward the beach gate that led to the boardwalk.

"Hang on and I'll go with you," Asher said. Billie heard his footsteps down the hall as he raced to go with her. She held the door open long enough for him to come through it, then let it slam shut behind him.

The panic inside her grew with every step they took toward the boardwalk. Billie stepped up on the wooden walkway that led to Rhonda's storefront, with her heart beating hard in her chest. When they arrived, they found the front door standing wide open and the furniture inside in disarray. She covered her mouth with her hand and stifled a scream.

Billie turned to see Asher standing at the end of the walkway with his phone pressed to his ear.

"She was supposed to come to the kitchen almost an hour ago," he was saying. Billie didn't have to ask. She knew Sully was on the other end. "The front door is standing wide open. Her desk is a mess, and everything was turned over."

Billie rushed inside the community center. They had not checked out the back of the space where Rhonda's private office was. She pushed through the door into the back and checked the bathroom first. The light was on, and the water still ran in the sink. Billie turned the water off and headed toward the office.

She pushed the door open, hoping to find Rhonda inside. Even if she was tied up and scared out of her wits, at least she would be there. The office chair was empty, the lights were off, and the computer was dark. Her friend was nowhere to be seen.

"Her phone," Asher said behind her. He pointed past her to the corner of the room behind the desk. Billie walked a little closer and bent down next to it. He was right. Rhonda's phone lay on the floor behind her desk. The screen had been cracked. Billie stood up slowly and turned back to Asher.

"He's got her," she said. Her voice was calm and even. "I know he's got her, and he isn't going to let her go."

CHAPTER 9

Alex stood in the middle of the kitchen space dusting sand off his white suit. Seeing him in the commissary kitchen, Billie was struck again how much he resembled old photos of Mark Twain. She wanted to be glad to see him. He was, after all, the reason she had everything her grandmother had left to her, but his visit to the island was not under happy circumstances. His presence without Rhonda close by reminded Billie of the deep panic she was in.

"This man, he is not an heir," Alex announced as soon as he spotted Billie in the hallway. "There is zero chance he has any claim on your inheritance, Billie. I have ordered my secretary to employ every investigator she can find to figure out who this man is."

"Thank you, Alex," Billie said. Her voice shook as she spoke. "I have no doubt we'll figure all of this out. I just hope it happens quickly."

Alex crossed the floor and stopped in front of her. She could smell cigar smoke and vanilla on his suit coat when he wrapped his arms around her. Something he had never done before in all his visits to the island. "We will find her," he said into her hair. Billie closed her eyes and allowed herself to melt into the grandfatherly figure embracing her. "It will only be a matter of time before Rhonda is found and home safe."

"Okay," Billie whispered. He released her from his embrace and waited while she dried her eyes.

"Your grandmother knew you would make a real go of this place when she had me draw up her will," he said, looking around at the expansive seating area and the state of the art test kitchens. "I can't imagine what Adeline would think of how far you have come. With only one more truck to go, you have proven yourself over and over with this small gift she left you."

"Small gift," Billie gasped. "There is nothing small about what my grandmother left to me. She gave me the chance to have a completely different life, and now look at what this has turned into."

Alex shook his head. "She left you her interest in the commissary kitchen and the festival grounds surrounding it, along with a dozen broken down old trucks and a little money to get started," he said. "But make no mistake, everything you see here is all because of you. That's the way she wanted it. She planned everything this way so you could prove to no one but yourself that you could do it. I know we're still just on the eleventh truck, but the test she set up was only for you to show yourself that you could make something out of the tools she left for you."

Billie took a step back. She was stunned and speechless. In the years since she had given up her life as a diner waitress in downtown Boston, Alex had never once given her so much detail about the trust her grandmother had left to her or the circumstances behind it. In the beginning, Alex told her there was something she had to prove in order to keep everything once the final truck was refurbished and underway, but until that moment, she had no idea what that test entailed.

"Thank you for saying all of that," she said quietly. She could feel the stirrings of relief and satisfaction deep in her soul, but she pushed it aside. She would have time later to celebrate, once her dearest friend was found alive and well.

"I'm going to my condominium for a little while," Alex announced. He placed a hand on her shoulder, then smiled his fatherly smile at her. "We will find Rhonda, and this clown claiming to be an heir to your grandmother's fortune will be found and tossed inside a cell. I promise you. When I return, we will go over some paperwork my secretary is sending me that will reassure you everything is fine. Okay?"

"Okay," Billie said. She managed another small smile. Alex turned back down the hallway past Asher's office. He walked with the gait of an old southern gentleman, then pushed the door open and let it shut behind him.

Billie sighed and hugged her arms around her middle. She hated the wait. The food trucks continued to operate outside. Asher had gone looking on his own around the festival grounds for any sign of Rhonda and asked for her to remain inside just in case she turned up. She had to do something, anything to pass the time.

Her office was the first place she thought to go. Billie sat down in her chair and pulled the lid of her laptop open. She tapped a few keys and stared at the screen, unsure what to even do. Maxwell Martin was clearly a fake name. No doubt his private investigator's license was as well. All she had of him that was real was his photo.

Billie opened her computer's files and searched for the photo. It was a long shot, but she might find something with a reverse image search. She uploaded it to the search engine and waited. Instead of a single good hit, the search returned dozens of social media profiles and advertisements for men's shaving products.

She could take the time to search through every profile and see what she could come up with, but her mind was too busy flipping through the worst case scenarios that were likely to be Rhonda's fate. She brushed hot tears from her eyes, feeling the rage building again. She slammed her hand down hard on the desk and began to cry.

"Whoa, what is going on in here?" Sully asked from the hallway. Billie looked up and wiped her eyes.

"What are you doing here?" Billie snapped. "I thought you were out looking for Rhonda."

"Upwards of twenty local and state officers are on this island at the moment searching everywhere for her," Sully said. She folded her arms over her chest and leaned against the door frame. "I came here for two reasons. One, I wanted to know what you've come up with on your own."

"At the moment, all I have is pages of search engine results to go through," Billie said. "I searched the image of Maxwell we had, and this is what that search returned." She moved the laptop around to show Sully the screen.

"Alright," Sully said. "That's a good start, but I do have some other information. We've located Maxwell's camper van. He had moved it from the marina parking lot. We did some looking around and found it parked behind an old building on the north-east side of the island. The place used to be a souvenir shop some years ago. We're waiting on a warrant to search the building right now."

"I guess that's something to go on," Billie said. "But you haven't said a word about Rhonda? Did you find her? Or any trace of her?"

Sully dropped her arms to her side and shook her head. "There's something else," she said. "We found blood inside the camper, and everything else had been cleared out."

"Including the zip ties and duct tape, I presume," Billie said. She closed her eyes and forced the tears back.

"We're doing the best we can," Sully said. "The

last thing is the name the van was registered under. It was not Maxwell Martin, and I don't think any of us were shocked about that fact, but there was another name, Max Long. I'm not sure if that is Maxwell's real name or if he stole the van from this guy, but maybe it is a place to start with those profiles you're looking through."

Billie nodded. She pulled the first page of profiles up and scanned through the names. By the fifth page, she sighed and sat back in her chair. "I feel like this is going to take forever," she said.

Sully pulled a chair out from the corner of the office and took a seat next to her behind her desk. "Can't you search the name and the photo at the same time?" she asked.

For a moment, Billie only stared at her. The simplicity of the question was almost appalling. She turned her energy and her concentration back to the computer screen and opened a second tab to the search page once again. She studied the page for a moment, then clicked on advanced search. "Bingo," she said. She uploaded the photo into the search bar once again, then typed Max Long in the secondary blank. A moment later, the man's ugly countenance stared back at her from the screen.

"I would say you found him," Sully said. "Let's

check out this profile and see what we can come up with."

CHAPTER 10

In the span of fifteen minutes, the entire area was filled with law enforcement agents. A dozen or so paced up and down the halls chatting amongst themselves in small groups. Billie remained behind her desk staring at the profile of the man who had threatened her and held the fate of her dearest friend in his hands. Max Long was his name. There was little doubt about it. She searched the photos of the man with thinning sandy blond hair and vacant eyes and wondered why he had chosen her.

How he had come to choose her was becoming clearer. His profile listed Gulfport, Florida as his hometown. His occupation was listed as a legal secretary. Sully and Chief Abernathy had left five minutes before for Alex Regent's beachside condo. They suspected that the man purporting to be the rightful heir of her grandmother's estate had actually worked for Alex's law office for a short amount of time.

Sully and the chief wanted to confirm those details with Alex, but the attorney was not answering his phone. Billie's reality felt paper thin when she'd watched Sully and the chief pull out of the front gate and head toward the main road. In the distance, she could see the top floors of the large condo building where she knew Alex was. She gazed at the building in the distance.

"The truck managers are shutting down for the rest of the day," Asher announced a second later. His words shook her out of her reverie, but the hollow feeling in the pit of her stomach was growing.

"Okay," Billie said. "Are you thinking about canceling the festival?"

Asher sighed. "I thought about it, but there's nothing going on here at the grounds to warrant it, so I don't think I will. Besides, most of the vendors are already on their way here. Chief Abernathy is worried about the extra people on the island in the coming days, but he has to balance that with the need to keep the tourism dollars coming in. Anyway, the food trucks are all shutting down, but…"

"Well, I'm glad the chief has his priorities in

line," Billie cut him off. "I sure hope Rhonda is on that list."

"Rhonda and her whereabouts are at the top of their priority list. They're just like us, juggling a whole lot of different things at once," Asher said. "Speaking of that, I have been trying to tell you, Cole is missing."

Billie opened her mouth again, but quickly lost her train of thought. "Wait, say that again."

"I said no one seems to be able to locate Cole," Asher said. "He was in his truck a short time ago, but Dillon did a quick spot check when he wouldn't reply to a text message and found the food truck empty and Cole nowhere to be seen."

"I, well," Billie stammered. "I have no idea what to do with that information."

"I do," Asher said. "I'm going to look over the camera feed to see if we can figure something out right away."

"In case we have another missing person?"

"Or an accomplice," Asher said. He breezed past her toward his own office. Billie quickly stood up from her chair and followed him.

"Why are you so sure Cole has something to do with any of this?" Billie said. "He's just a pastry chef."

"And where is this Max guy from, Billie?"

Billie closed her eyes and exhaled. "Gulfport, but that doesn't necessarily mean anything," she said.

Asher opened his office door and flipped on the lights. "Okay, and where was Cole living?"

"In the same area, but that doesn't mean they're connected," she said.

"They are already connected, babe," Asher said. He immediately sat down in front of the camera monitors set up in his office.

"How are they connected?" Billie asked. Asher held up a single finger while he opened his laptop and rewound the footage for the camera with the best view of the donut truck. He stopped the footage and pressed pause, then turned to Billie. "If Max, whatever his name is, worked for Alex for a short time and Cole was handpicked by Alex to be your next food truck manager, they are connected. Alex is the connection." He turned his attention back to the monitor and rolled the footage.

Billie said nothing more. She stood behind Asher and watched the screen. For several moments, they watched as customers came and went to the donut truck. Enid's mousse truck was parked next to it. Enid had not opened her truck up for the day as she planned a day off while she prepared for the festival.

Four minutes into the footage, Cole appeared to see something off in the distance. "There," Billie said. Asher paused the recording. "Did you see that? He was looking at something. Go ahead and play it a little while longer."

Asher clicked play and watched. "He sees something," he said. Twenty or so seconds later, Cole's arms gripped the frame of the order window. Immediately after that, he retreated from the window and ran through the side door off in the distance toward the same direction he had been so intently watching.

"Where is he going?"

"I don't know," Billie said. She was breathless from the adrenaline pumping through her veins. "See if you can get another view. Same timestamp."

Asher fumbled with the other cameras. "The view isn't great, but this is the general direction." He rewound the footage and froze the frame. "There!" He stood up and leaned in for a closer look.

"You're in the way, Asher," Billie said. "I can't see anything."

Asher stepped back out of her way and pointed to the grainy image on the screen. Billie squinted for a better look. "I see two people, a man and a woman," she said as she studied the image. "Is he holding her arm? It looks like he's got her arm behind her back. Asher!"

"Yeah, same thing I thought, too," he said. "That looks like Rhonda and Max. This was less than two hours ago."

"We have to call Sully," Billie said. She pulled her phone out and dialed the detective's number. "We have another problem. My new truck manager Cole is missing, and when we looked over the footage, we think we captured an image of Max and Rhonda together. It looked like he was getting rough with her."

"It also looks like Cole caught up to the two of them," Asher added. He rolled more video footage. "He confronts them and then he follows them off screen."

"That's not the only problem we have, you guys," Sully said quietly. Billie had the phone on speaker mode. She leaned in a little closer to hear the detective's voice.

"Sully," Asher said. "What's going on?"

Sully sighed and cleared her throat before she could answer. "I'm afraid we have some very bad news, and I would not be telling you this over the phone but in light of what is going on…"

"Just tell us what's happening," Billie interrupted.

"I'm afraid when we got to the condo, it was too late," she said. "We found Alex on the floor."

"Oh, gosh," Billie said. "Did you call an ambulance? Is he speaking?"

"Listen to me," Sully said. Billie heard the sound of a door closing behind her. "Alex is gone. There was a necktie wound around his neck. I'm afraid he's no longer with us."

CHAPTER 11

Moments later, Billie found herself looking up at Asher, who hovered over her with his hands reaching down to pick her back up. She reached for him, grateful for his help.

"What happened? Billie, Asher?" Sully's voice echoed in the small office. After steadying her on her feet, Asher picked up her phone and turned off the speaker. Billie sat in his desk chair and halfway listened while he turned away and spoke.

"She's alright now," Asher said. "I think it hit her pretty hard." He continued with a few comments about the bombshell the detective had just dropped on them.

"So, it's true?" Billie asked. She felt the first wave

of tears hitting her. Alex Regent was dead. The man who had contacted her years before and told her about the enormous, generous gift her grandmother had given her was gone. Along with Rhonda, Alex was the only remaining link to her grandmother.

"What happened over there, exactly?" Asher asked. Billie couldn't hear Sully's reaction on the other end of the line, but she imagined her words were filled with the sordid details of his death. Despite her initial reaction, Billie decided she did not wish to stick around and listen. She stood up and began her walk down the hallway toward her own office.

Just before the call came from Sully, they had watched Cole take off from his food truck. She had three huge issues pressing in on her. One was Rhonda's disappearance. The second, of course, was the revelation of Alex's death, something she had yet to fully take in. But Cole's disappearance was the one she had the least information about. It was also the one thing she felt she could do something about.

She opened her laptop and began searching through Max Long's social media profiles. She was sure they had the right guy. His piercing eyes had a way of jumping off the screen. Billie looked away several times as she scrolled through his photos.

Billie looked a little further into Max online. She scrolled through more than just the photos on several social media platforms. After a while, she started to form a picture of the man. Post after post showcased his dreams, from trips to exotic destinations to flashy cars. Some posts were captioned "when do I get mine" and "why are some privileged while others can only dream." More recently the posts took on a darker tone.

Whatever his real name was, Max was a man with a chip on his shoulder. Billie returned to the photos. She scrolled back as far as she could go and found a younger version of the man, active and smiling in several photos. "What else are you into, Max?" she asked.

The answer came quickly. Billie found several posts with Max and a handful of smiling friends seated on the edge of a boat ready to fall overboard with their snorkels and flippers on. He was into diving. In other photos, the same group of friends posed in front of the mouths of large caves.

Sully had assumed that the zip ties and duct tape in his camper van had been meant for cave exploration or some other form of outdoor adventure. Billie wondered if that was the story he had given the police. She picked up her phone to call Sully and ask but hesitated. The detective was rather busy at the moment, still processing the crime scene at Alex's island condo. She stopped and waited as a fresh round of sobs overtook her for several moments.

When she got control of herself at last, she stood up and shook her head. As much as she wanted to collapse into a fit of grief, she still had to do whatever she could to save Rhonda. It was her only mission. She looked around her office for a moment, searching for a direction. She could visit local dive shops or wander down to the beach and see what she could see. She stepped out of her office and rushed back towards Asher's. What direction had Cole been headed? She could start there.

"Billie, where are you going?" Asher called after her.

"To the beach," she said. "I have a thought."

"Wait!" Asher hurried to his feet and went after her. "What do you think you're going to do?"

"I don't know," she said as she rushed out the door and across the sand. "I have to do something because sitting around here isn't helping anyone. The police are busy at Alex's condo, you know."

"Okay," Asher said. He reached out and grabbed her arm. "Stop for a second and talk to me. What are you thinking?"

"I'm thinking Max Long had a real desire for wealth and riches, and that turned into hatred of people who had more than he did," she said and described the posts she had found on his social media profiles. "I think he used to be active and then his life changed for whatever reason. He sought me out because he found out about my inheritance while he worked for Alex's law office. Whatever possessed him to come here and try to claim it was all his, I have no idea, but I don't think he's operating with a real plan. He's unraveling, and that's why he killed Alex."

"And why Rhonda and Cole are in grave danger," Asher said.

"So, you no longer think Cole is involved?" Billie asked.

Asher shook his head. "No, and if you had seen the rest of the surveillance footage, you would understand why," he said. "He was trying to stop Max from taking Rhonda when he spotted them. You could hear him yelling off camera, trying to make him let her go."

Billie closed her eyes. Cole Rodrigo was not a criminal secretly collaborating with the unhinged stranger. He was simply a good man who saw someone in danger and tried to stop it. She hoped that the day's death toll would stop with one.

"Why were you headed to the beach?" Asher asked her. "Tell me what you were thinking. We probably don't have a lot of time."

Billie swallowed hard. "The south beach. Maxwell was into scuba diving and spelunking," she said.

"What the heck is spelunking?" Asher asked.

"Caves, exploring caves," she said quickly.

Asher's face lit up with her words. "The south beach," he said again. "There have been cops all over this island and nothing turned up. You might have just figured everything out."

When they reached the remote sand dunes on the southern tip of the island Billie picked up her speed.

"Asher," she said breathlessly and pointed to the outcropping of rock on the far side of the dunes.

Something lay on top of the rock. They raced closer. "It's clothing."

"Yeah, it looks like it was just left here," Asher said. He bent over for a closer look. "That's a woman's sweater."

"Why would there be a woman's sweater sitting out here in the middle of nowhere?" she said. "I think that's Rhonda's. She's the only person I know who wears a sweater around her waist even during the hottest parts of the year."

Asher took her by the hand and led her further up the rocks. Water rushed below them. "How good of a swimmer are you?"

"I can hold my own," Billie said. She began removing her shoes while Asher unfastened his belt. He picked up his phone and quickly dialed.

"South beach, rock face and caves," he shouted into the phone, then set it carefully on the rocks beneath his shoes. With a wink and a smile, Asher grabbed her by the hand once again and led her over the edge of the small cliff. They landed in the clear water below and started exploring the front of the rock face. Asher said nothing but pointed downward and bobbed up in the water long enough to inhale a long breath, then disappeared beneath the surface of the water.

Billie followed suit. She swam quickly behind him. About ten feet down, he grabbed her hand again and signaled to a small hole in the rock. He released her hand and headed in. Billie swam in right behind him. They broke the surface in a large air pocket inside a small cave. She filled her lungs with air and looked around.

"Asher!" she screamed. A pair of legs was visible

about twenty feet from the opening. Together they
made their way over the rough cave floor and pulled
the body from the rocks. Once again, hot tears
streamed down her face. She knew the clothes, and
the one shoe remaining on her feet. It was Rhonda.

"Her face wasn't in the water," Asher said. He
strained to carry her back to the mouth of the cave
where the sunlight above streamed in.

Billie picked up her legs and helped him carry her.
When he gingerly set her down, she rushed to the
older woman's side. "Rhonda, can you hear me?" she
cried, patting her face and head.

"She's breathing," Asher said. "We have to get her
help."

"What about Cole?" Billie asked. "Do you see any
sign of him?"

"Over there." Asher pointed.

Billie looked up from Rhonda. She could see the
outline of a man standing in the distance where the
cave ceiling rose up over the floor. "That isn't Cole,"
she whispered.

Asher pointed down at Rhonda. "She's coming
to," he said, then looked back at the figure on the
other side of the cave.

"Rhonda," Billie said. She quickly rubbed the

older woman's shoulder. "Can you sit up?" Rhonda nodded her head and raised up a little.

"Take her and head for the surface," Asher said. He did not take his eyes off the advancing figure. "Go, Billie. Get help. Go now!"

Rhonda's eyes widened as the man in the darkness advanced. Asher stood up and blocked the women. Billie said nothing, but pulled Rhonda to her feet and halfway dragged her to the mouth of the cave. She sucked in a deep breath and grabbed Rhonda. Rhonda gave her a little nod and filled her own lungs with air, then launched herself alongside Billie toward the surface.

A few seconds later, Billie broke through the water. Rhonda followed close behind. She gasped for air. Billie rushed to her side and helped her remain afloat.

"We have to get the police," Rhonda whispered.

"Asher called them before we headed down," Billie said. She looked around for a stretch of beach they could easily access. Rhonda was weak and shivering in the water. "This way." She pulled Rhonda's hand toward the shore. Even if they had to swim along the rocks, the extra support would buy Rhonda some time.

"Billie!" Sully called out to them from the top of the bluff.

"Down here," Billie called up. "We need help! I have Rhonda with me. Asher is still down below. Max is down there, too."

"Over this way," another officer called out. Billie spotted the beach and pulled Rhonda along with her as fast as she could. He reached down and helped Rhonda to her feet. Billie exhaled when she spotted two paramedics waiting for them.

"I have to go back and help him," Billie called out to Sully.

"You can't," Sully said. She tried to navigate over the rocks and down to the beach. "You just helped Rhonda to the surface, Billie. You're in no shape to go back."

"He's down there by himself," Billie said. She walked toward the water's edge again. "I can't leave him down there with that man. He's a killer."

"We know," Sully said. "We have proof he killed Alex."

"What about Cole? Have you located him?"

"I'm afraid that we haven't been able to find him," Sully said. "We have divers headed this way. They will be here in a matter of minutes."

"Asher may not have minutes," Billie cried. She walked out into the water and began to swim toward the rock face above the cave, but before she could fill her lungs with air, Asher broke the surface of the water. He yanked something up with him.

CHAPTER 12

Billie was seated on the back of the ambulance wrapped in a towel. She leaned against Rhonda who was also wrapped up to help keep her warm. Asher stood on the beach with Sully, who was leaning in to listen closely to his account of what happened below the surface.

"Hold on a second," Sully said. Another police officer tapped her on the shoulder and called her away.

Billie looked over to the second ambulance where a still unconscious Max Long lay handcuffed to a gurney.

"I wonder if he's going to make it?" Billie asked.

"Is it bad if I say that I hope he doesn't?" Rhonda

asked. She pulled the blanket up around her shoulders and stared at the ground.

"Did he hurt you?" Billie asked her.

Rhonda shook her head slowly. "I don't remember anything after we hit the water."

"Do you remember anything about the cave?"

She shook her head again. "Not until I came to, and you guys were down there," she said. "How did you know?"

Billie shrugged her shoulders. "Social media, photos on his profiles," she said. "I knew he was into diving and caves at one point in his life."

"Now he's just into hating people," Rhonda said. "He is a bitter, terrible man."

"I figured that out from his online presence, too," Billie said. "That's why he targeted me."

"And Alex," Rhonda said. Billie's eyes widened at the mention of his name.

"I know, Billie," Rhonda said softly. "Max bragged to me about killing him. I'm so sorry. He was such a good man."

"I know," Billie whispered. "I don't know what we're going to do without him."

"You're going to keep on running this business like your grandmother knew you could, that's what."

"Billie," Asher called out to her. "They found something."

Billie hopped off the bumper of the ambulance. She waited while Asher made his way over to her. He was smiling ear to ear. "What are you talking about?" she asked. "What did they find?"

Sully made her way toward them. "We found Cole," she said. "He's alive. He's injured, but alive. They're bringing him up now."

Billie slumped against the side of the ambulance. "I'm so glad," she said softly. "I am just so glad."

"Ms. Knapp," one of the paramedics came around the other side of the ambulance. "I think we should take you in and have you checked out."

"Are you talking about the clinic or the hospital?" Rhonda slid to her feet and faced him. She wavered for a second. Billie rushed forward to catch her. "I think you need to go to the hospital," she said.

"Your friend is right," the paramedic said. "You've suffered a serious blow to your head, and we don't know how long your breathing may have been compromised."

"Okay, yeah," Rhonda said. "But I'm still expecting that meal you promised me, Billie." She allowed herself to be guided into the back of the ambulance.

Billie stood next to Asher while the ambulance doors closed behind her, and the ambulance pulled away. "I can't believe we got her back," she said, leaning her head on Asher's shoulder.

"We didn't get her back," Sully said. "You did this. The two of you. I should have listened to your instincts. Maybe Alex would still be alive."

"We don't know that," Asher said. "Besides, like you said before, you did everything you could within the law."

Sully nodded her head. "Yeah, but we all know how close to that line I can come," she said. "I should have pushed the line a little harder."

"You can't beat yourself up," Billie said. "We don't know how he might have reacted if you had."

"She's right," Asher said. "Pushing him too hard may have resulted in more death and destruction."

A noise on the other side of the rocks cut off their conversation. Billie rushed to the edge of the beach. She watched as two divers guided Cole to the soft beach. His eyes fluttered as they carefully pulled him onto the sand.

"Here's the real hero," Asher said. They stood back as paramedics rushed in to care for him. He held onto Billie while they lowered a gurney and helped Cole onto it.

"I don't think the donut truck is going to be operational in the morning," Sully said.

"I'm not so sure about that," Billie said. "I saw the way he made those malasadas. I think I could run it for a few hours at least."

"You want some help?" Sully asked.

"Why, are you looking for some part-time work?" Asher asked her. "I thought the cupcake truck had your heart?"

"Actually, I'm going to take a page out of Agent Malloy's book," she said, referring to the federal agent who had recently been in their lives. "Between this situation and everything else that has happened since I've been on this island, I think it's time that I take some time to myself. Starting tomorrow, I'm taking a six-week hiatus. I think it would be nice to pitch in and help out until Cole is back on his feet."

Billie cast a sideways look at Asher. "Are you sure?" she asked. "It's an early morning, and a lot of prep work."

Sully watched as they loaded the gurney onto the third ambulance. "I don't love them, but I can manage some early mornings," she said. "I think I owe Cole one or two of those."

"You're not the only one," Asher said. "I thought he was in cahoots with the bad guy."

"So, it will be the three of us," Billie said. "Together. We'll run the donut truck while Cole recovers."

"Hopefully not into the ground," Asher joked.

"No way," Billie said. "The chief better watch out, though. If he's not careful, we're going to poach his best detective to run a truck of her own."

***

If you enjoyed A Real Jam and are looking for more food truck adventures, preorder The Bitter End, today!

AUTHOR'S NOTE

I'd love to hear your thoughts on my books, the storylines, and anything else that you'd like to comment on—reader feedback is very important to me. My contact information, along with some other helpful links, is listed on the next page. If you'd like to be on my list of "folks to contact" with updates, release and sales notifications, etc.… just shoot me an email and let me know. Thanks for reading!

Also…

… if you're looking for more great reads, Summer Prescott Books publishes several popular series by outstanding Cozy Mystery authors.

CONTACT GRETCHEN ALLEN

Visit my website for more information about new releases, upcoming projects, and be sure to check out my special Members Only section for extra freebies and fun!

Website: www.gretchenallen.com

Email: contact@gretchenallen.com

Visit the Summer Prescott Books website to find even more great reads!

Made in the USA
Coppell, TX
09 June 2023

17906346R00067